For Nicky

Freddie the Fly

by **CHARLES GRODIN**

illustrated by **SAL MURDOCCA**

Random House New York

Text copyright © 1993 by Charles Grodin. Illustrations copyright © 1993 by Sal Murdocca.
All rights reserved under International and Pan-American Copyright Conventions.
Published in the United States by Random House, Inc., New York, and simultaneously in Canada
by Random House of Canada Limited, Toronto.

Library of Congress Cataloging-in-Publication Data
Grodin, Charles.   Freddie the fly / by Charles Grodin, illustrated by Sal Murdocca.
p.   cm.   SUMMARY: While traveling with his parents to visit his grandmother, Nicky befriends a fly
that helps him out when he's in trouble.   ISBN 0-679-83847-3
[1. Flies—Fiction. 2. Friendship—Fiction.] I. Title. PZ7lG89247Fr 1993 [E]—dc20 92-5234

Manufactured in the United States of America   10 9 8 7 6 5 4 3 2 1

Nicky and his parents were riding in a big limousine to the airport. They were going to visit Nicky's grandmother in Kansas City.

"Look," Nicky's dad said.

Nicky's head shot up. "What?" he asked.

"A fly," said his dad. "Look, Nicky, there's a fly in the car."

Nicky looked around, and sure enough, he saw a little fly flying around the big, big car.

"I think he's going to Kansas City with us," his dad said.

"Kansas City?" Nicky asked.

"Yes," his dad said. "I think he'll ride with us in the car to the airport, and then get on the plane and fly with us to Grandma's."

Nicky giggled.

In the airplane, Nicky saw a fly sitting on the window watching the clouds outside. He smiled and pointed to it. His parents nodded and chuckled.

"What do you think his name is?" his dad asked.

Nicky thought a moment. "Freddie," he said. "I think his name is Freddie the fly."

When Nicky, his parents, and Freddie got to Grandma's, there were kisses and hugs all around from Grandma and Nicky's cousins and uncle and aunt—all except for Nicky's older cousin, Roy.

When Roy saw Freddie, he grabbed a fly swatter and tried to hit him.

"No, no!" Nicky cried out. "That's Freddie. He's my friend."

Roy snorted. "You have a fly for a friend?"

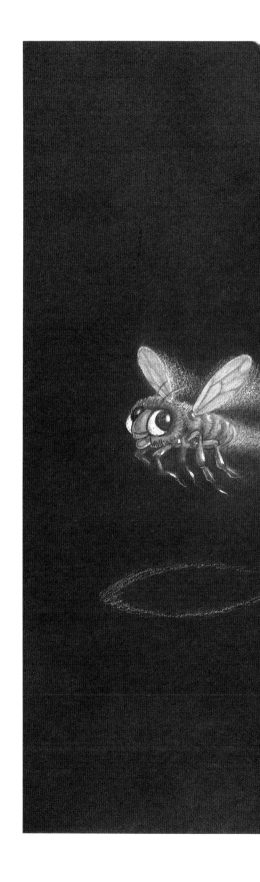

Later that day, Nicky was out in Grandma's backyard, swimming in the pool. And there was Freddie sunning himself on Nicky's raft. When Roy saw Freddie, he splashed water and tried to drown him. But Freddie flew to a poolside table and just grinned at Roy.

That night, when Nicky went to sleep, there was Freddie
sleeping on the windowsill beside him. Just knowing Freddie
was there made Nicky happy.

Nicky was Freddie's guy and Freddie was Nicky's fly.

The next day, Nicky went to the playground with his dad and Cousin Roy. Freddie flew off to a nearby cornfield and made some new friends, Harry and Harvey, a couple of Kansas City flies.

Harvey and Harry introduced Freddie to the bee boys—
Billy, Bernie, Barney, and Blue. They flitted about the cornstalks
and shot the breeze.

Meanwhile, back at the playground, Roy was saying, "I dare you to walk up the slide. Bet you can't."

"I'd rather slide down it," Nicky said.

"That's 'cause you're a baby. A crybaby. A *fly*baby! That's what you are!" And he started to shove Nicky around.

Nicky wanted to be brave, so he didn't call for help. But Harvey the fly, who was flying over to the playground for a drink of water, saw what was happening and flew back to the cornfield to tell Freddie.

When Freddie heard that Nicky was in trouble, he and the two Kansas City flies zoomed to the playground, where Cousin Roy had just knocked Nicky down. Nicky's dad was busy reading the newspaper and wasn't aware of what was going on.

Freddie and friends buzzed Roy and tried to make him stop.

"Get lost, fly!" Roy said, and swatted Freddie, sending him hurtling backward into a rosebush.

Freddie lay there for a second, dazed, then looked up and saw four bees taking pollen from a rose. They were his new friends, the bee boys— Billy, Bernie, Barney, and Blue!

Meanwhile, Roy had pinned Nicky to the ground. Harvey and Harry were still buzzing around Roy's head, but they were getting tired.

Nicky struggled to get up when suddenly he heard a buzzing sound.

He looked over Roy's shoulder and what did he see but a fly, *his* fly, Freddie the fly, leading a dive-bomber attack of bees headed straight for Roy!

Cousin Roy leaped to his feet as Billy scored a direct hit. He let out a yelp and ran from the playground with the bee boys buzzing after him.

Freddie checked to see if Nicky was okay. The grin on Nicky's face said he was *more* than okay.

That evening, Grandma had a barbecue. Freddie, Harvey, Harry, Billy, Bernie, Barney, and Blue played in the bushes. When no one was looking, Nicky threw them a glazed sparerib.

Everyone had a wonderful time, except for Roy, who had to sit on a pillow.

The next day, Nicky and his parents flew home. There was Freddie, on the window again, watching the clouds.

Nicky smiled. He had a new friend, and he knew that, no matter what trouble came his way, Freddie would be there to help. It would be a foolish person who ever gave Nicky trouble...

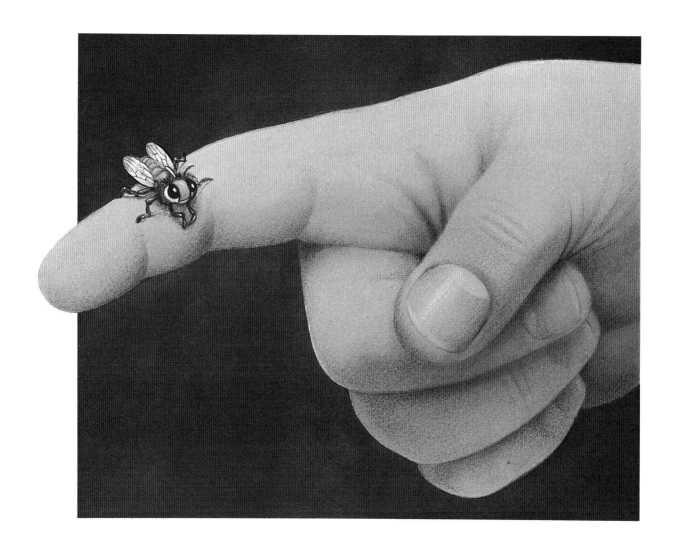

...because Nicky was Freddie's guy
and Freddie was Nicky's fly.